Samuel Ilwar

Racing rhymes on turf topics

The thoroughbred

Samuel Ilwar

Racing rhymes on turf topics
The thoroughbred

ISBN/EAN: 9783337271770

Printed in Europe, USA, Canada, Australia, Japan

Cover: Foto ©Andreas Hilbeck / pixelio.de

More available books at **www.hansebooks.com**

RACING

RHYMES

ON

TURF TOPICS, THE THOROUGHBRED, ETC., ETC., ETC.

BY

S. N. ILWAR

NEW YORK
GOODWIN BROTHERS
1440 Broadway
1899

DEDICATION.

To ALL ye faithful "Regulars," who journey to the track
Day after day, through sun and storm, your favorites to back;

To all ye pleasure loving souls, who "care not for the game
So much as for the thrilling sport"—but play it just the same;

To all ye worthy owners, who run races "on the square"—
About the other kind of course I really do not care;

To all ye great officials, stewards, judges—powers immense—
Also ye mighty starters and ye "rail birds" on the fence;

To all ye jolly bookmakers, who work so hard to get
A very small percentage from the public—who will bet;

To all ye journalistic scribes, who for the papers write
Those full reports in which the sporting public delight;

To all ye anxious trainers, who use so much care and thought
That your charges to the post in prime condition may be brought;

To all ye gallant pigskin knights, who give a straightout ride
And always try to win, whatever horse ye may bestride;

To all ye careful hostlers, rubbers-down and stable boys,
And everybody else that this grand enterprise employs;

To all ye students who delve deep in records, "form" and "dopes,"
To whom a Good-win is a thing on which ye pin your hopes;

To all ye winsome fair ones, who delight to view the races,
And brighten up the grand stand with your toilets and your faces;

In short—to everey one who loves the "sport of kings" so great,
And loves the noble thoroughbred, this book I dedicate.

CONTENTS.

CONTENTS—Continued.

JIMMY AND SNAPPER AND FITZ.

JIMMY AND SNAPPER AND FITZ

"And there were Giants in those days."

YOU may tell of your heroes who
  meet in the ring,
 Your Sullivans, Corbetts and all,
 But the Knight of the Pigskin's
  "the baby for me,"
And he on my muse "has first call."
Yes, if he's a "Cracker-Jack" you may be
  sure
He can show as much courage and nerve
As any bold warrior who in the brunt
Of the battle his country might serve.
His eye must be keen and his wit must be
  sharp,
For he has but a moment to choose
'Twixt one course or the other, full many a
  time,
Which a fortune may win or may lose.
And of all the brave boys who to saddle have
  jumped

In those contests of speed, pluck and wits,
There are none more deserving of undying
    fame
Than "Jimmy" and "Snapper" and "Fitz."

Sturdy Jimmy McLaughlin, your name ever
    stands
Interlinked with the names of a few
Of the most famous horses we ever have
    known,
Who always were mounted by you:
Miss Woodford and Kingston and Hanover
    too,
Queen and kings of the turf in their day,
Again and again have you steered them safe
    home.
While the best of the others gave way.
A steady, square ride was the kind you put
    up,
And good judgment was in it all through;
If you failed to get first there was rarely a time
When the blame could be placed upon you.
So the "Red with Blue Sash," when you came
    on the track,

Was ever a glad sight to see;
And your name should be known while a race
      track remains
In our land of the brave and the free.

Hurrah for "The Snapper!" that youth debon-
      nair,
So lissome and graceful and trim,
Who rode like a lightning streak flashing
      through air;
There were none who could "snap" it like
      him.
When his mount might have won by a few
      open lengths,
He would make it appear by his art
That he worked like a Turk just to win by a
      nose.
And a daisy he was at the start;
For he'd stand still and watch for a chance
      to rush through,
And crawl up, and sidle, and back,
And play every trick that a jockey can try
Till they gave him the best of the track;
Then—zip!—he was off, and the others would
      break,

And the flag dropped, and he had the lead.
Yes, the "Garrison finish" still blazons his
    fame;   ·
Ah! he was a <u>jockey</u> indeed.

Dare-devil Fitzpatrick! The name in itself
Brings up from the depths of the past
A legion of memories, stirring and strong,
Like the sound of a war trumpet's blast.
Those races snatched out of the jaws of de-
    feat
By riding so dashing and wild,
That it seemed like the work of a desperate
    fiend,
Or a man by a demon beguiled;
Those hair raising squeezes close in by the
    rail,
Where a shadow could barely get through,
But where the bold boy saw the ghost of a
    chance
And seized it with eye keen and true.
Alone in his style stands the "Dare-devil"
    jock,
No other can match him therein;
He'd take every risk that presented itself,
With only one thought: "I must win."

The days have gone by when this trio so
    great
Thrilled the hearts of the whole racing world;
New idols are raised and adored for a while,
Then down from their altars are hurled.
I would not disparage the merits of those
Who shine as star jockeys to-day;
There are many among them well worthy of
    fame,
Whose names on the records will stay.
Yet for me there are none who can hold such
    a place,
And around me can throw such a spell,
As the three I have named, and thus feebly
    have tried
Of their glories a little to tell.
And so, when my memory far from me strays.
And as through the dim past it flits,
It returns o'er and o'er to the soul stirring
    days
Of "Jimmy" and "Snapper" and "Fitz."

DERBY DAY.

DERBY DAY.

———◆———

LONDON'S streets seem very quiet;
  Looks like Sunday "down on
    'Change;"
  All the clubs have lost their mem-
    bers;
Something's happened—very strange!
What on earth can be the matter?
Ha! I just heard some one say
"Half the city's gone a-racing"—
Why, of course. It's Derby Day!"
    *   *   *   *   *

Out upon the road to Epsom
Fifty different kinds of rigs;
Four-in-hands and hucksters' wagons,
Tilburys and doctors' gigs,
Donkey carts and blooded turnouts;
Liveries and toilets gay,
Rags and tags—all bound for Epsom;
You might know it's Derby Day.

What a dust they all are raising!
Yet the crowd don't seem to care;
Jolly jokes and bursts of laughter
Ring upon the soft spring air.
Fashion's beauties smile at beggars;
Folly holds despotic sway;
Social lines seem sadly shattered
By the power of Derby Day.

In that vast procession, wending
On its way to Epsom Downs,
Every face seems bright and sunny;
One may look in vain for frowns.
Though the road is badly crowded
And the rich man's drag gives way
Very often to the poor man,
None complain—it's Derby Day.

When the course is reached, how stirring
Is the scene that meets the eye!
Shows the games of every nature,
Tricks and trades both low and high;
Countless schemes to catch a penny—
"Try your luck here!" ye who may;
"Never mind a 'bob' or 'tanner'!" *
Blow it in—it's Derby Day.

*Shilling or sixpence.

Flower girls vend their fragrant posies:
"Lady, buy my roses sweet!"—
And some haughty, fair patrician,
For whose decking would be meet
Rare exotics, priceless orchids,
Buys a shilling's worth in play;
Pins them on her filmy laces;
Quite en regle—Derby Day.

Swarthy Gipsy fortune tellers
Seek the future's book to read
On the palms of stately beauties,
Who of "fortunes" have no need.
Bands of tuneful Wandering Minstrels
Sing some merry roundelay,
And "the hat" ne'er passes vainly;
'Tis well filled on Derby Day.

Mountebanks and clowns and jugglers
Vie in feats of every kind.
Charity is, too, a feature:
"Help the cripple!" "Help the blind!"
Few are they who grudge a penny;
Pleasure sheds a kindly ray
O'er the hearts of those who feel the
Influence of Derby Day.

As the vital hour approaches
When the great event is run,
Thrilling waves of deep excitement
Stir the heart of every one.
Look upon the eager faces,
Young and fresh, and old and gray,
All aglow with expectation
Of the race of Derby Day.

Betting waxes fast and furious;
Wagers of all kinds are made,
From the bonbon stakes of fair ones
To the fortune that is played
By the bold, adventurous plunger.
None escape the powerful sway
Of the speculative fever
Which prevails on Derby Day.

Now the doughty equine champions
Sally forth toward the start.
Cheers ring out for each contender;
Jockeys, too, receive their part
Of the multitude's applauding,
Which to each one will convey
Nerve and courage for the struggle
Now at hand, of Derby Day.

Then there comes a curious stillness
O'er the erstwhile noisy throng;
Breathless, all await the moment
They've looked forward to so long.
Soon a mighty roar arises,
Like a tempest dashing spray,
And we know the race has started
Which gives name to Derby Day.

Oh! those few all fateful moments!
Myriad hearts are beating fast.
Well it is that such emotion
Can for but a brief space last!
None could long endure the tension;
Strongest nerves would soon give way
Under such o'erwhelming pressure
As that race of Derby Day.

Ah! It's over! One's first feeling
Is a sense of deep relief.
Though to some comes exultation,
And to many comes but grief.
Some are richer; some are poorer;
One has gained fame that will stay
With him always—'tis the owner
Of the horse of Derby Day.

Plaudits greet the noble winner,
That great horse whose worthy name
Will from henceforth stand forever
On the turf's high roll of fame.
Even losers swell the greeting
When the hero comes to weigh,
And receive the azure guerdon,**
Trophy proud of Derby Day.

'Tis a great and grand experience
Such a glorious scene to view;
And, to me, a recollection
Which will last my whole life through.
Wonderful! how those brief moments
O'er a people's hearts hold sway!
Ah! a mighty institution
Is Old England's Derby Day!
    London, 1879.

**Blue Ribbon.

SUBURBAN DAY

SUBURBAN DAY.

With Apologies to the Manes of Tennyson.
(The word "manes" is not meant as a horse pun.)

YOU must wake and call me early,
    call me early, Johnny dear;
  For to-morrow will be the great-
    est day of all the racing year.
Of all the racing year, Johnny, the
  crasiest, wildest play;
For to-morrow's Suburban Day, Johnny, to-
  morrow's Suburban Day.

There'll be ten or fifteen starters, Johnny; each
  one has got a chance.
To try and pick the winner, Johnny, it puts me
  in a trance;
For there's five or six I'd like to play—but I
  cannot play them all,
So I guess I'll take the "longest" odds, and
  make my bet quite small.

No, I won't put up on the favorite, Johnny, for
    I always feel as if
The "public money" in <u>that</u> race will make
    the best horse "stiff."
With Eurus and Loantaka and Tillo in my
    mind,
I'll back some rank outsider, and just simply
    go it blind.

There'll be a fearful crowd, Johnny, and all will
    want to bet.
The "Holiday Pikers" will rush around for
    any odds they can get.
The bookies will reap a harvest if the favorite
    doesn't win,
For the public will put up on him the limit of
    their tin.

They'll fight and squeeze and push and jam to
    get their money down,
And the ring will be like Donnybrook Fair or
    a mob let loose in town;
Yet for all their rush and hustle at the odds to
    get a whack,
The chances are that few of them will get their
    money back.

I'm awful glad Suburban Day comes only once
    a year :
For I will tell you something. Johnny, and it is
    rather queer:
I've played the races many years, and my hair
    is turning gray,
But I never could win a dollar on any
    Suburban Day.

So that's the day I cut away from "handicaps"
    and "dope,"
And simply in the foolest kind of luck I place
    my hope.
On other days I try to bet in a scientific way,
But I shut my eyes and "stick a pin" when it
    comes Suburban Day.

Then call me early, Johnny dear, and we'll go
    and get a drink;
And we'll breakfast very leisurely; and we
    won't try to think
Of handicaps or weights or form, and we'll put
    our "dope" away,
For to-morrow's Suburban Day, Johnny, to-
    morrow's Suburban Day.

BOTH WAYS.

BOTH WAYS.

PETE PLUNGER was a "Regular,"
   A "Handicapper" smart,
   Who knew the records of the turf,
   And knew them all by heart.

He'd tell a horse's pedigree
   If you but gave his name,
And tell of every race he'd run,
   And if he'd won the same;

He'd tell the weight that he had up,
   The jockey on his back,
The distance of the race, and the
   Condition of the track:

He'd tell the odds that there were laid,
   The horses that were in—
In short, he could tell everything
   But some sure way to win.

And even on that doubtful point
  He would explain to you
A brilliant "system" that he had,
  Quite certain to "go through."

The only things you had to have
  To make his system work
Were fifteen thousand dollars and
  The patience of a Turk.

It chanced that Pete had got one day
  A "dead sure" "inside tip,"
And joyfully he started for
  The track—his daily trip.

He visited his bank and drew
  A roll of money out,
To bet upon this "leap pipe cinch,"
  Without a single doubt;

Because, not only had he got
  The tip so sure and straight,
But he had also "figured out"
  That horse's chance as "great."

And he was ready to declare,
  By all the gods of "dope,"
That only this one horse could win,
  The others had no hope.

Now as upon the boat he went,
  En route the track to reach,
He met his old friend, Franklin Fresch,
  Bound for Manhattan Beach.

Most highly pleased were both to meet,
  For mighty friends were they;
Though each one found his fun in life
  In quite a different way.

Pete cared for nothing but a race
  Where he could make a bet;
Frank scarcely had a race track seen,
  Nor backed a horse as yet.

But Frank would walk ten miles to see
  A pretty girl and flirt,
While Pete thought less of female charms
  Than so much common dirt.

Yet as the boat sped fast along,
 They sat and talked apace,
And Pete told Frank, in confidence,
 About this "cinchy" race.

"Say, Frank, my boy," said genial Pete,
 "You'd better come with me
Down to the track and play that race,
 You'll sure a winner be."

"I'd like to go first rate," said Frank,
 "If I had not, perforce,
To meet a lady at the Beach;
 She must not wait, of course."

"But, then," cried Pete, "this race is first,
 And when it's run you'll go
Down to the Beach and meet your girl;
 She's sure to wait, you know."

Thus urged by Pete, Frank said at last
 That at the track he'd stop,
Provided it was certain that
 No money he would drop;

"For, Pete," said he, "while I am sure
　　Your tip looks very good,
This betting business is by me
　　But little understood;

"And if I lost upon this race,
　　'Twould make me feel quite bad;
Besides the risk that I shall run
　　Of making my girl mad."

"No fear that you will lose!" cried Pete,
　　"Your sure to win a pile!
And then your girl, e'en though you're late,
　　Will softly on you smile."

So then into the train they passed,
　　And to the track did hie;
Frank up into the grand stand went;
　　Pete to the ring did fly.

He soon returned with glowing face,
　　And whispered in Frank's ear:—
"He's favorite! He has been backed!
　　He's sure to win—no fear!

"I've put five hundred on myself;
    What shall I bet for you?
You'd better put up all you can,
    You'll never better do."

"Well, Pete," said Frank, "I've only got
    Just sixty here in all;
But take the cash and put it up.
    I don't want to seem small."

"All right, my boy," said Pete, "that's good!
    And though I've played mine straight,
I'll put your money on 'both ways,'
    That's safe, as sure as fate!"

Then to the ring Pete runs again,
    Soon comes back very gay,
And, giving Frank a ticket, says,
    "You've thirty on each way."

The horses now are at the post;
    The "good thing" acts quite bad;
He plunges, kicks and bucks around;
    It must be "dope" he's had.

There is a weary, long delay;
   The "good thing" will not start.
The starter jumps down from his stand
   And uses all his art.

He rushes out upon the track
   And waves his flag, and swears;
For starters as a rule, you know,
   Say anything but prayers.

At last he gets them all in line,
   And jumps back on his stand.
"Now, if they'll only break!" cries Pete,
   "Our start will just be grand!"

There is a break; the flag goes down,
   "They're off!" the crowd all yell;
But Frank hears, hissing in his ear,
   Pete's exclamation, "H—ll!"

And out upon the track he sees
   The "good thing" run—alone;
But not the way the others run,
   They far away have flown.

For as the starter dropped his flag,
   The "good thing" wheeled around
And ran the wrong way of the track,
   His backers to confound.

And many an angry groan goes forth,
   And many a muttered curse,
And many a man is thinking of
   His amputated purse.

Poor Pete himself is wild with rage,
   And loudly vents his ire;
Then turns around to comfort Frank,
   Whose pluck he does admire.

For Frank has never said a word,
   But smiles with face serene,
While Pete expected that he'd be
   With consternation green.

He laughs at Pete's grim, rueful face,
   And cries, to Pete's amaze,
"Sorry for you, but I'm all right!
   My bet was made 'BOTH WAYS!'"

FIFTY TO ONE.

FIFTY TO ONE.

E jumped out and beat the flag, sir,
   And opened up a gap
Of half a dozen lengths, sir,
   Under a "double wrap."
   Then I held my ticker tighter,
For it looked like a good thing;
'Twas only 100 to 2, sir,
   But I felt just like a king.
I shouted "They'll never get near him!
   "My horse they'll never ketch!"
But he faltered on the turn, sir,
   And "blew up" in the stretch.

He finished an awful last, sir,
   And I threw my ticket away.
I felt confounded bad, sir;
   'Twas such a likely play!
The jockey that was on him, sir,
   Is my pertic'ler friend;
He told me they had backed him, sir,
And he'd ride "from end to end."

Besides the trainer told me
   That he wasn't out for fun,
But was "tryin' " for a "killin';"
   And the price, sir!—Fifty to One.!

THREE GREAT BABIES.

THREE GREAT BABIES.

THESE are the days when youngsters
  have the call
  And infant prodigies the Turf con-
   trol;
  The horseman's greatest hope seems
   now to fall
Upon the future of some unseen foal.
That ancient proverb, "Do not try to count
 Your chickens ere they're hatched," is ob-
  solete;
The richest golden flood from fortune's fount
 Flows toward some unborn colt who'll be
  most fleet.

The grand "Futurity," that glorious prize,
 And countless other two-year-old rich
  stakes
Hold forth their tempting bait before the eyes
 Of each ambitious owner; and he takes

More pains, and feels more pride, and spends
　　more cash
　To get a possibly great two-year-old
Than e'er he would some record fast to smash.
　Thus is the Turf by youngsters now con-
　　trolled.

Of all the many infants of this kind
　Who have been public idols in their days,
A few there are whom specially we find
　Worthy of lasting fame and loudest praise;
And three of these stand out from all the rest
　So grandly prominent in their career,
So fully equal to the hardest test,
　That we are fain to sing their praises here.

———◆———

HIS HIGHNESS.

(Ran as a Two-Year-Old in 1891. Won $108,000.00.)

Grand sounding and patrician is the name
　　Of this great horse; and he did not belie
His title, but did well uphold the same
　　In those fierce contests which his speed did
　　try.

Son of a "Princess," precedence he took
　In a most literal sense, for when he ran
No one in front of him his pride would brook,
　And at the finish he <u>would</u> lead the van.

In his imperial two-year-old career,
　Up to "six figures" did his winnings mount;
Record but few can show; and hence 'tis clear
　He should among the great immortals
　　count.
Yet we do not lucre homage pay
　Or on mere gain bestow the highest meed;
We praise His Highness in the sportsman's
　　way
　For stamina and pluck and splendid speed.

Now from the Turf's most active life he's
　　passed,
　And as a sire is gaining honors new;
His offspring have his courage and are fast,
　And glorious deeds we look for them to do.
He is in worthy hands, for we are sure
　That, placed among the magnates of the
　　sport,
His present owner's fame you'll find secure
　In all good ways which Fortune's blessings
　　court.

DOMINO.

(Ran as a Two-Year-Old in 1893.   Won $180,000.00.)

"Black Whirlwind" was the title thou didst
    gain,
    And nobly didst thou win it through that
      burst
Of overwhelming speed, which, in thy strain,
    Stands out above all other things the first.
Gameness thou hadst, and stamina as well,
    Coupled with gentleness and temper mild;
For all thy greatness, I have heard them tell
    That thou couldst have been ridden by a
      child.

Rich was the winning which thy triumphs
    made—
    A fortune in itself—a mighty sum!
High on the golden list it stands displayed,
    To be the wonder of all years to come.
But thy proud owner, man of ventures vast,
    Of iron nerve and enterprise supreme,
Thought more of thee than wealth that thou
    amassed;
    Thy gains to him did but a trifle seem.

Thus, when thou passed away, his sorrow deep
  Moved him to rear thee a memorial stone,
Which stands above the spot where thou dost
    sleep,
  To tell the world how all thy virtues shone.
Great son of Himyar, thou dost stand alone,
  And while the records of the turf shall last
Thy fame the topmost place should surely
    own;
  It might be equalled—could not be sur-
    passed.

— ◆ —

JEAN BERAUD.

(Ran as a Two-Year-Old in 1898. Won $70,000.00.)

The latest star that gloriously doth rise
  To dim the other meteors of speed
Is Jean Beraud, a colt in whom there lies
  An inborn power of highest type indeed.
Son of His Highness, whom we here have
    named,
  Well qualified by ancestry is he
To hold the place he's gained and be far-famed
  Through such a lineage of proud degree.

Fortunate, too, is he, in that his lot
  Is to be owned by one whose honored name
Lends to the Turf that lustre which is not
  Brought save by those who spotless records
    claim.
When he who wisely steered our ships of state
  Gave to the sport his countenance and
    means,
Every true turfman's heart felt pleasure great,
  Because such aids ennobles racing scenes.

So let us, to this latest brilliant star .
  Wish all success in his career to be,
To spread his name abroad, both near and far,
  That all the racing world his fame may see.
Worthy is he to rank with Domino
  And with His Highness—more cannot be
    said;
"For these few words his greatness fully show
  And rank him as a wondrous thorough-
    bred."

L'ENVOI.

Think then of these great three—of others,
  too,
  Proud, well known names on which we fain
    would dwell,
But that a volume's space would scarcely do
  Should we essay of all such stars to tell.
Then it may be that we will, one and all,
  Say it is well, as on the seasons roll,
That these are days when youngsters have the
  call
  And infant prodigies the Turf control.

PAROLE.

PAROLE.

— ✦ —

(Dean Swift, in writing of the Houyhnhnms, makes us infer that
horses have souls. The writer believes so, at all events.)

——✦——

LET me tell again how old Parole—
      Bless his soul!—
Raced for honor of his native land,
Far away upon a foreign strand.
Let me tell again how well he won—
      Nobly done!—
While our English cousins all exclaimed
That to lose they did not feel ashamed,
When a gallant horse like old Parole—
      Bless his soul!—
Beat their best ones hollow; "For," said they,
"Such a horse we don't see every day."

Our good English cousins saw Parole—
      Bless his soul!—
In their "City and Suburban" race,
Show their thoroughbreds a winning pace.

It was nearly twenty years ago;
       But I know
That it seems like yesterday to me
When I journeyed forth that race to see.
I had heard that plucky old Parole—
       Bless his soul!—
Was to start in their great race that day,
And I went my country's horse to play.

So I put my cash on old Parole—
       Bless his soul!—
While my English friends stood by and
    laughed,
And my "Yankee Cheek" they gaily chaffed;
"Ah," said they, "now do you really think"—
       With a wink—
"That your Yankee horse can beat our
    cracks?
He can't run upon our English tracks!"
"Well," said I, "I like our old Parole—
       Bless his soul!—
And I love my native Yankee land;
And my bet is down—so there I stand!"

Soon the race was off; and old Parole—
       Bless his soul!—

Came along as steady as a clock,
And as solid as old Plymouth Rock,
Rating on with honest measured pace
   Through the race,
Till the finish came, and then he shook
Off the others one by one and took
The lead. Then roared I "Come on, old
  Parole!—
    Bless your soul!—
Show them what a Yankee horse can do!"
"Hail Columbia!" and "Red, White and
  Blue!"

Past the winning post dashed old Parole—
   Bless his soul!—
And behind him followed England's best.
Patriotic fervor swelled my breast,
And I shouted "Now, boys, don't you
  think"—
    With a wink—
"That our Yankee horse, on English tracks,
Can hold his own with some of England's
  cracks?
Here's three cheers for honest old Parole!—
   "Bless his soul!"—

My English friends joined in them loud and
     strong;
For generous thoughts to English hearts
    belong.

Yes, they cheered for gallant old Parole—
     Bless his soul!—
And we went and drank his health in wine,
Until I felt as if the world were mine.
Glory to our glorious land!—
     May it stand
First in racing, as in everything!
Honor to the sportsmen kings who bring
Forth such horses as our old Parole—
     Bless his soul!—
Who upheld the colors that he bore
And brought them back in triumph to our
    shore.

THE GENTLEMAN TOUT.

THE GENTLEMAN TOUT.

— ◆ —

WILL you kindly let me glance upon
        your card, sir?
        I've dropped mine somewhere
        down here in the ring."
        I turned, and at my shoulder
    stood a stranger,
    With look and dress and manner "quite the
        thing;"
His words were with the most politeness
        spoken,
    His face expanded in a gentle smile—
A perfect gentleman he seemed, most surely,
    And guileless as to any trick or wile.

I handed him my card; he scanned it quickly,
    Cried "Ah! I thought so!"—then he gave
        it back
Saying, "Thank you, sir," and turned away
        and left me,
    Going out beyond the ring, toward the
        track.

Five minutes later, once again I saw him;
　　He nodded to me with a knowing wink,
As to a book maker some words he uttered;
　　The bookie smiled—it was good news, I
　　　　think.

Then stepping to my side he softly whispered,
　　"I'm feeling pretty sure what horse will win;
In fact, I've just had first class information
　　That lightning fast his latest work has been;
I also know the stable's backed him heavy—
　　His price has just gone a point or two;
And so I've just put up my last cent on him—
　　I thought I'd like to give the tip to you.

"The reason that I asked to see your card, sir,
　　Was that a friend of mine, a week ago,
Told me "The Kempton Stable" had a gelding
　　Who soon would win—my friend is "in the
　　　　know."
I noticed by your card "The Kempton Stable"
　　Own Parachute, and then I rushed, of
　　　　course,
To see this friend of mine, and when I found
　　　　him
　　I asked him if that was the proper horse?

"He told me that it was, and also urged me
    To play it hard, and added then besides
About his work, and how the stable backed
        him:
    I went and interviewed the boy who rides,
Whom I know well; he told me that his or-
        ders
    Were to make every post a winning one,
And that in warming up his mount he'd
        noticed
    That he was fit, and very full of run.

"So I made up my mind that I would press it,
    And, as I said, have just bet my last cent,
Which I would never do unless quite certain
    The horse I backed was "fit" to win and
        "meant."
Then seeing you, remembering your polite-
        ness,
    I thought that for it I might make return
By telling you about this information
    Concerning Parachute, which I just learn."

In those days I was innocent and "easy;"
    And he seemed such an honest, pleasant
        chap,

I swallowed with avidity his story—
　　Even as a toothless infant swallows pap;
So, though I had already backed "my fancy"
　　For "five each way," which was my usual
　　　　stake,
I went and put on Parachute a "Fifty,"
　　Determined that I'd either make or break.

My new found friend stood by me while I
　　　　bet it
　　And heartily approved of what I'd done;
Then said he'd meet me when the race was
　　　　over,
　　When he supposed I'd feel like "standing
　　　　one;"
To this I very joyfully assented,
　　Whereon he left me "to look up a friend,"
While I, to see the race, from out the ring
　　　　went
　　And up into the stand my way did wend.

The start was quickly made—the race was
　　　　over—
　　And Parachute was never in the hunt;
But my own choice, on whom I bet ten dollars,
　　Won easily, and always was in front;

Forty I won on him, but that just left me
　Ten dollars out on the whole blessed thing,
And feeling very sore about that "Fifty,"
　I started to go down toward the ring.

While standing on the stairs, I saw before me
　My "friend" who had on Parachute gone
　　　broke;
He did not notice I was there behind him,
　And thus I heard some words he gaily spoke
Unto the man who by his side was walking:
　"Well, didn't I <u>tell</u> you that he'd surely win?
I hope you put a good big swell bet on it
　And feel like letting me for some stand in!"

When I heard this it fazed me not a little:
　I had some faint suspicion of the game:
And later on I met a friend and told him
　About the chap, and well described the
　　　same;
It happened that just then I once more spied
　　　him,
　And to my friend the man I pointed out;
He cried "Oh! that's your precious fellow,
　　　is it?
　He's nothing but an "All Round," "Sure
　　　Thing" Tout!"

THE DARK SKINNED TOUT.

THE DARK SKINNED TOUT.

SAY, boss, I sees yo' gwine ter
  play, sah;
  Jest step er leetle bit dis way,
  sah.
Ef yo' am gwine ter play Jim Hood, sah,
I tells yo' dat hoss ain't no good, sah.
   Come awa-a-ay!
   Don' yo' pla-a-ay—
Don' play nuthin' but what I say!

"Wha' fur yo' play on dat ole hoss, sah?
Dat hoss kain't win dis-yere race, boss, sah.
Lem'me put yo' on; I kin give yo' de winner;
Ef I don', yo' kin call me er doggone sinner.
   Come awa-a-ay!
   Don' yo' pla-a-ay—
Don' play nuthin' but what I say!

"Yo' see dat mar'? She'll be de winner;
Dey's layin' ten ter one agin her;

Jest go an' put five on dat mar', boss;
She'll win, an' win it right–smart far, boss.
                    Come awa-a-ay!
                    Don' yo' pla-a-ay—
Don' play nuthin' but what I say.

"My ne'vew work in dat mar's stable;
He say dat mar'es sure 'nuff able
Ter show her heels ter de hull bilin',
An' fer er race she's jest er spilin'.
                    Come awa-a-ay!
                    Don' yo' pla-a-ay—
Don' play nuthin' but what I say!

"He work dat mar' de oder mornin',
Befo' de day wuz done er dawnin';
She runned de quarter in twenty-t'ree—
Ain' dat enuff fer yo' an' me?
                    Come awa-a-ay!
                    Don' yo' pla-a-ay—
Don' play nuthin' but what I say!

"Wha'-wha'-wha's dat yo' say ter me? "Git
        out!" boss?
I tells yo' dat I ain't no tout, boss.

Ef yo' don' wan' ter take dis tip, sah,
Go an' lose yo' money-an' I'll jest skip, sah.
   Go awa-a-ay!
   Don' yo' play-a-ay—
Don' play nuthin' dat dis chile say!"

THE TOUGH TOUT.

THE TOUGH TOUT.

L OOK 'ere, mister, lemme tell yer
  Dat dis bloody roice's fixed.
  Don't yer go 'n lose yer boodle
   An' wid all dem jays get mixed;
  Let er cove wot "knows it" tell yer
De best t'ing yer ever see—
Den go in 'n sock it heavy,
  An' put sunthin' on fer me.

"Dan McGinnis, on de Bowery,
  Runs er gin mill—know 'im well—
Las' night, w'en we wuz er' lushin'
Got ter feelin' fine 's 'ell.
'E stan's in wid all dese trainers,
  An' 'e sez ter me, sez 'e,
"Petey, I kin make yer fortin,
  If yer'll keep it dark now, see?"

"Den I sez, sez I, "I'm fly Dan,
  Wot yer tells no furder goes.'
An' he flashes out dis good t'ing,
  An' de trick ter me 'e shows;

All de hosses in dis bizness
 Is dead stiff ter Jumpin' Jack;
'E's de hoss dat's got ter win it,
 'E's de only hoss ter back.

"All de jock 's goin' ter lally,
 An' let Jumpin' Jack walk in;
All dem odder hosses' trainers
 On de Jack has got deir tin;
An' 'e's goin' ter get de start, too;
 Fur de boys hez got down;
Dat't wot Dan McGinnis telled me,
 W'ile de drinks 'e passed aroun'.

"I wuz goin' ter play dis good t'ing,
 But I wuz er bloomin' chump;
Los' me money on de fust roice—
 Put 't all up in er lump.
T'ought dat fust roice wuz er lay-down,
 An' I'd git er wad ter bet
On dis cinch—an' lemme tell yer,
 It's er moral!—don't forget!

"I don't ought ter give dis tip out,
 Dan wud smash me fer dis play;
But I'm broke an' wan' ter bet it;
 T'ought I'd put yer on de lay,

'Cause I seen yer bet 'em heavy,
  An' I t'ought yer'd stake me, too.
Go 'n put er hun'red on it!
  Dis 'ere job's er goin' t'rough.

"Wot! Yer've got anodder hoss played?
  Hully Gee! Dat makes me sick!
Go 'n get dat money off, now!
  Make er sneak 'n get it quick!
Fur de hosses is er goin'
  To de post—don't lose yer chance!
Change de bet ter Jumpin' Jack, boss!
  Dis 'ere ain't no song and dance!

"Wot! Yer goin' ter stan' pat, den,
  W'en yer know about dis job?
Den go put five on fer me, boss—
  Pay yer back, so 'elp me Bob!
Wot! Yer ain't er goin' ter do dat?
  W'en I've telled yer 'bout dis t'ing?
Well, yer sure to lose yer money,
  Fer yer up agin "De Ring.""

TWO KINDS.

TWO KINDS.

T HE race was done. I stood upon
    the lawn,
    Gazing about me at the moving
    throng.
    Nothing cared I which way that
  race had gone;
For, while I never was a bettor strong,
On that event I had not bet one cent,
And, as I said, cared not which way it went.

It really was amusing to remark
The various expressions on the faces;
From barn-door grins to frowns like midnight
    dark,
As gain or loss had left their varying traces.
Almost each man whose looks my glances met
Apparently had made his little bet.

One gay young swell was hurrying toward the
    ring,
A fellow dressed in Fashion's latest mode;
He looked as happy as a new made king
Or like a man who never tailor owed;
Within his hand a ticket close he held;
With winning pride his shirt-front fairly
    swelled.

Just as he passed me by he met a friend,
And stopped and slapped him gayly on the
    back,
Saying in tones that all the air did rend,
"Hurrah! Look here! You bet I've got 'em;
    Jack!"
And to his brother swell, like him arrayed,
His ticket he triumphantly displayed.

"Heavens!" thought I, "he must have hit it
    hard;
A hundred dollar bet he must have booked!"
And as the distance was about a yard
I cautiously upon his ticket looked.
The winner's price was eight—that much I
    knew;
Our young friend's ticket read—"16 to 2."

Near to my side had stood throughout the
     race
A plain old man, one rather roughly clad,
Who showed no sign upon his hard-lined face
That any interest in the race he had;
And as I once had looked this man upon
He seemed, like me, only a looker on.

The finish was a close one; and so hot
That, till the winning numbers were displayed,
No one could tell which horse the race had
     got.
The old man then one quiet question made:
"My eyes are getting rather old to see;
Tell me, sir, is that top one 5 or 3?"

He, too, had marked the scene the swells be-
     tween
And marked the winner's exultation wild;
Then, as they hurried off along the green,
He turned around to me and grimly smiled.
"It's hard," said he, "to see how some folks
     win;
I can't get that much pleasure—dang my
     skin!"

So saying, down his hairy, brown hand went
Into his trousers pocket, and brought out
A bunch of tickets, crumpled up and bent.
Thought I, "They're losing ones, without a
      doubt.
For his old face looked solemn as an owl,
And his remark was something like a growl.

He counted out those tickets, one by one,
Slowly and carefully. I, looking on,
Could scarce believe my eyes when he had
      done   .
And quietly toward the ring had gone.
Twenty-three winning tickets did the old man
      get;
Each one a fifty or a hundred dollar bet!

THE BOOKYMONSTER.

THE BOOKYMONSTER.

EWARE! Beware! Avoid his lair!
    He thirsteth for thy money.
He lies in wait within that gate,
    By yonder course so sunny.
He'll lure thee on with cunning
        tongue
In his sweet odds to revel,
That of thy cash he may make hash
And send thee to the devil.

Look out! Look out! There is no doubt
    If once his spell o'ertakes you,
Your purse he'll seize and he will "freeze
    You out" until he breaks you.
Your every cent for him is meant
    If once you let him charm you;
Therefore take heed while thus I plead,
    "Stay off" and he won't harm you.

THE TRUE BOOKMAKER.

THE TRUE BOOKMAKER.

OH! a jolly old soul is the bookmaker;
    Yes, a jolly old soul is he,
As he smiles on his box
While he handles his "rocks,"
    With his gallant assistants three.

Oh! a crafty old soul is the bookmaker;
    See him finger his bit of chalk,
As he "marks 'em up" here,
And he "marks 'em down" there,
    While he gives you his cunning talk.

Oh! a nervy old soul is the bookmaker;
    For he often is forced to play
In a desperate game,
Where a slip, if it came,
    Would sweep him and his money away.

So he needs all his wits, does the bookmaker,
    When the plungers are after his cash;
And e'en his own kind,
He will frequently find,
    Have been plotting to send him to smash.

But an honest old soul is the bookmaker;
   If you happen to hand him a "roll"
Which exceeds what you bet,
You are likely to get
   Back the surplus—he'll not keep the whole.

And a kindly old soul is the bookmaker;
   His hand is e'er open to aid
A friend who's in need;
None in vain to him plead
   If a good, honest case they have made.

So, take him all 'round, the <u>real</u> bookmaker
   Is an excellent kind of a man;
He need cause no alarm,
For he does much less harm
   Than your brokers and stock-jobbers can.

And though, now and then, there's a book-
      maker
   Who brings disrepute on his class,
By some action not "white"
Or some trick that's not right,
   'Tis but rarely he's found—let him pass.

So, when people sneer at the bookmaker,
   They are showing how little they know;
For his record's as fair
And his life is as square
   As "the odors of sanctity" show.

THE START.

THE START.

HUMING, fretting and curvetting;
　　Fifteen horses at the post;
　　Half a dozen of them "bad ones;"
　　　Hard to tell which kicks the most.
　　Starter swearing, little caring
Whether he is heard or not.
His assistant, whip persistent,
　　Stirs the boiling equine pot.

"Now, you jock there! run a block there
　　Will you, when you break again?"
Then that kid receives a blessing
　　In choice words, which I won't pen.
"Here now, Billy, don't get silly!
　　Turn your horse's head around!
Or I'll bet you I will set you
　　Down upon the cold, cold ground!

"Jack, come up there! Lash that pup, there,
　　Sam, if he stays back like that!—
Well, if this don't beat the devil!
　　What's got into you, now, Pat?—

Sam, just catch him! Wish they'd scratch him
   Or refuse to let him run—
That d—d kicker! Come! Get thicker!
   Line up, bless (?) you—every one!

"Are you ready? Now there! Steady!
   BREAK!—Confound your blooming eyes!
What d'ye mean by standing still there?—
   Such a monkey I despise!"
By this token, all have broken
   But one horse, who still hangs back;
Gone the rest are, and the best are
   Now half way around the track.

While returning, language burning
   Greets that jockey whose hard fate
Finds him mounted on the sulker
   Who has caused the start to wait.
E'en they fine him, or consign him
   To the ranks of those who walk;
And he's lucky, that same duck he
   Is, to get off with a "talk."

Once again they group, and then they
   All their tricks and kicks renew;
While the starter, getting madder,
   Lets himself out "not a few."

Fines them plenty—ten or twenty—
   Even fifty—sometimes more;
Or suspends them, and that ends them
   Till "the powers" their rights restore.

Weary waiting—crowd belating;
   Bettors anxious; judges cross;
Everybody quite disgusted;
   Starter, even, at a loss.
Horses skipping—Sam keeps whipping—
   Will they <u>never</u> get away?
All revolting, kicking, bolting;
   Looks like they were there to stay.

Now they gather. That's good, rather;
   Only one or two still lag.
Starter gives a final caution—
   "Now look out there!"—lifts his flag—
"GO!" They've started! Off they've dart-
     ed;
   Not together—for a part
Go a-sailing—others trailing;
   Pretty bad! But it's a start!

THE FINISH.

THE FINISH.

ROUND the turn, with a desperate
    dash,
Into the stretch they swing.
Seven horses are all abreast.
Flying as if a-wing.
Every jockey is riding with vim;
With tight set teeth and with visage grim;
The stake is rich, and a win for him
Will be a glorious thing.

Thousands of pairs of eager eyes
Are watching them "straighten out;"
Thousands of hearts are throbbing fast
With fear or hope or doubt.
The plunger's plunge and the piker's bet
Alike in the balance hang as yet.
For none can tell who the race will get
In such a hard fought bout.

Four of the seven falter and fail,
Falling back to the rear;

One of the others forges ahead,
Making his backers cheer.
He, the favorite, sticks to the rail,
But the other two are at his tail,
Their jockeys riding with tooth and nail;
Any one's race, 'tis clear.

One of the rear guard comes again,
Catches the leading three;
A rank outsider, and all unbacked,
Any one there can see.
All the cheering dies out and ends;
Only the bookmakers and their friends
"Call on" the horse who now contends;
No favorite is he.

The leader's jockey draws his whip;
The bookies loudly yell.
The rank outsider gains inch by inch;
His jockey rides him well!
Falls the whip on the favorite's flank;
His backers' faces look dazed and blank;
Their hopes of winning suddenly sank
When that one whip stroke fell.

Now they are fighting it neck and neck;
Only a few yards more!
The favorite gets his head in front;
His backers give a roar;
His jockey, the crack boy of the day,
Lifts his horse in a masterly way;
Every muscle is put in play;
Game is he, to the core!

Yet the outsider hangs grimly on.
"If better jock were there,
He'd win, and win it easily!"
The "rail birds" all declare.
But a premier jock the favorite rides;
He gets in his work in the last few strides,
And like a flash past the wire glides—
Wins the race—"by a hair!"

HOW CLARA DIDN'T BET.

HOW CLARA DIDN'T BET.

OW—let—me—see. Who starts in
　　this? I really do not know
What I shall play. Dear me! my
　　programme's lost! Where did
　　it go?
I'll have to buy another one. No, here it is!
　　How nice!
It makes me feel so cross to have to buy a
　　programme twice.
Now—let—me—see. What's number six?
　　I always look there first.
Good lands! it is that horrid horse that's
　　owned by Mr. Hearst;
I wouldn't bet a cent on him, for—only
　　think!—one day
He beat a horse that I had played, though it
　　led all the way;
That's made me hate him ever since. But I
　　like "Number Six,"
For that's my lucky number. Oh! there's
　　Tom! He always picks
Such splendid winners! Come here, Tom, and
　　tell me what is good.
You like that horse of Mr. Heart's? I didn't
　　think you would.

Now it is just an awful shame for you to tell
    me that;
Because you know I will not bet on him—and
    that is flat!
Do tell me something else. You can't? Then,
    sir, you just can leave.
How you can like that mean old horse I really
    can't conceive.
Now—let—me—see. Here's Sweetheart in.
    That's such a lovely name
That I believe I'll bet on him; it will be all the
    same,
For any horse can come in first; and—oh!
    there's Mrs. Pike!
I'll speak to her. Say, Mrs. P., do tell me
    what you like.
You like that horse of Mr. Hearst's? Good
    gracious! it's too bad!
Every one likes that nasty horse but me. It
    makes me mad.
And he's my lucky number, too! Perhaps I
    ought—but no;
I'll bet on anything but him, because I hate
    him so!
Now—let—me—see. Here's Lucky Dog; he
    won one day last year;

Maybe this year he'll win again—Oh, boy!
     please come up here!
(Those stupid boys are all so slow!) Who's
     favorite down there?
That wretched horse of Mr. Hearst's! Well,
     I will just declare!
Seven to five? It seems to me those odds are
     very small;
Why, if he won you'd scarcely get back any-
     thing at all.
What's Sweetheart's price? Fifteen to one!
     Now isn't that too nice!
I'd like so much to win a bet at such a lovely
     price;
I'd buy myself a new silk dress, and—Now—
     just—let—me—see.
I'll look at my programme again. No, boy;
     don't wait. Here's three
Other nice names; I like them all. Japonica—
     that's sweet!
And Love's Delight—how nice that is! And
     here's Flying Feet.
Such pretty names! But then I think that
     Sweetheart is the best;
I guess I'll make a bet on him; he ought to
     beat the rest.

Why, goodness me! They're at the post! Oh,
    dear! Where is that boy?

I'll lose my chance! If I don't bet, the race I
    won't enjoy.

There! They are off! I told you so! And
    Sweetheart is ahead.

He's going to win! It's just my luck! Re-
    member what I said!

See that old horse of Mr. Hearst's; he cannot
    run a bit!

He's nearly last. My stars! this thing almost
    gives me a fit!

They're in the stretch; see Sweetheart run!
    I'm sure he's going to win;

If I had only bet on him, how glad I would
    have been!

Oh! what is that? That horrid horse of Mr.
    Hearst's is next—

He's catching Sweetheart! Now, just look!
    He's gaining! How I'm vexed!

That old horse wins! And only think! Tom
    told me I must get

Nothing but him! And Mrs. Pike! I'm sure
    that way she bet!

It's just too bad! I'm positive, if that boy had
    stayed there

I would have put my bet on him. It almost
    makes me swear!

LOOK ON THIS PICTURE

AND THEN ON THIS

LOOK ON THIS PICTURE

---◆---

ALL the crowd are gayly cheering
When the favorite wins.
And there's wining and there's
beering
When the favorite wins.
And the bookies all are paying,
And the bettors smart things saying,
And they're anxious for more playing
When the favorite wins.

---◄•►---

AND THEN ON THIS.

◆ -

THERE'S a silence and a sadness
When the long shot wins.
There's a crowd that's sour to mad-
ness
When the long shot wins.
And the bookies all are smiling,
And with jokes the time beguiling,
And with cash their boxes piling
When the long shot wins.

LEFT AT THE POST.

LEFT AT THE POST.

POUND him? Well, my dear feller,
 you'd better bet your life!
As hard as any drunken longshore-
 man ever pounded his wife.
I had in my clothes altogether just
 one hundred and seventy-five;
And I put it all on—every dollar—as sure as
 you're alive.
I felt so dead sure of winnin' that if I could
 have pawned my socks
I'd have put that money up besides. Why, he
 would have won by blocks;
For there wasn't a bit of a question but what
 he was the best hoss
And trained to the minute. And backed?—
 like there couldn't be no loss.
Only a few of us good ones—Tom's friends—
 were "in the know;"
By George! if we had pulled it off how we'd
 made the champagne flow!

They opened him up at sixes and we backed
    him down to threes;
And four or five of the bookies got pretty
    weak in the knees
And refused him altogether. Tom put fifteen
    hundred up,
And told me his hoss would win sure. Con-
    found that dirty pup
Of a starter! He had five good breaks, at the
    least;
And Tom's hoss was always jumpin' out like
    a bullet that is greased,
And the others all got off well too; but he
    wouldn't drop the flag;   ·
Looked to me like he wanted to favor some
    other feller's nag.
Anyway he kept 'em standin' there for just
    about half an hour,
While Tom was a-cussin' and swearin' for all
    that was in his power;
Because his colt is nervous, and likes to get
    away quick,
And if he's fussed about at the post sometimes
    he won't run a lick.
For all that Tom's jock had orders to drive
    him for all he was worth,

And sure he was fit that very day to beat any-
    thin' on earth;
Besides, the kid had on himself a fifty dollar
    bet
And a couple of hundred from us boys was
    pretty sure to get.
If they'd waited even another half hour, and
    then given him a show,
There wasn't one in that field but what he
    could have made look slow;
But when that fool of a starter dropped the
    flag and gave the word
(It wouldn't have pleased him very much if he
    could have only heard
What Tom and us fellers called him), our hoss
    was standin' flat,
With his head turned round the other way;
    and I will eat my hat
If the others weren't a sixteenth off before he
    could get around.
Then that skin of a starter says to our jock,
    "Now, sir, you can stay on the ground
For a week, because, with the others you
    wouldn't try to break."
Holy Moses! but that was the worst of all!
    The dirty bloomin' fake!

To burn up our good money, and then lay the
    blame on our jock!
It's good I wasn't at the post; I'd a hit him
    with a rock;
Or anyway I'd a-cussed him hard. No matter
    what they done.
Let 'em rule me off if they wanted to! The
    sneakin' son of a gun!
Well, it's over, and I'm busted. If you've got
    a dollar to spare
Let me have it till to-morrer, for I only paid
    my fare
One way, and I don't feel now much like want-
    in' to walk back
To the city and go without supper after gettin'
    such a crack.
For I can stand most anythin' and never turn a
    hair;
I can lose my money by a nose, and you'll
    never hear me swear;
I can get on a "stiff" or be t'rown down and
    drop a pile of tin,
Or have my hoss "pulled" out of the race—and
    you'll only see me grin.

But there's one swipe I can't stand at all, and
    it knocks me in a heap;
And makes me want to tear my hair, and cuss,
    and swear, and weep;
For I feel like a man who's just been hung
    and sees his grandmother's ghost
When I back a hoss that couldn't lose—and
    see him LEFT AT THE POST.

PUER STABULI.

SCENE FROM

THE TRAGEDY OF

"PUER STABULI"

("THE STABLE BOY")

---

*(The manuscript of this tragedy is supposed to have been discov-
ered in the ruins of the hippodrome at Pompeii; and the same,
in a fragmentary condition, is now in possession of the
author, who has made a very liberal translation from
the Latin of the following scene, found in some of
the best preserved portions of the manuscript.*

CHARACTERS:

JIMICIUS MACORMICUS,...........A Roman Trainer.

TODDIO SLOANIO,..................A Popular Roman Jock.

SAMBONIUS NIGER................A Rubber-Down.

PUER STABULI,................ ....The Stable-boy.

(NOTE—It is a singular thing that while this tragedy is
called " Puer Stabuli," " The Stable Boy," and while he is supposed to be the principal character, yet he never really appears
upon the scene as a speaker in any of the parts or fragments of
the Latin manuscript which the author has in his possession.
The author believes, however, that this same idea has obtained
in several other antique tragedies and comedies, whose writers
have named the same after some character who never really
appears on the stage in a speaking part.)

ACT II. SCENE I.

———◆———

Evening, A Track Stable; Stalls with Horses, Buckets, Blankets General Racing Stable Paraphernalia.

JIMICIUS MACORMICUS. (Alone, and seated upon an inverted bucket; his head leaning upon his hand; musing in deep thought.)

Jim Mac.—An incubus rides on my mind to-
    night,
  Yet can I not unfathom what it is.
  The stars all tell me something is not right,
  And still methinks I understand my biz.
  (Calls) Sambonius! Without, there!

[Enter Sambonius Niger.]

Sam.—   Yes, Mars' Jim.
Jim Mac.—Have all the horses had their usu-
    al feed?
Sam.—Yes, sah; deys all done eat fust rate but
    him (points to a horse);
  He wouldn't take no oats, indeedy-deed.
Jim Mac.—Ha! This is strange!
        (Aside.) There is some mischief here.
  (To Sam.) Was any stranger snooping
    round to-day?
  And have you kept close watch?
Sam.—   Yes, sah; dis yere
  Ole coon hab not one minnit been away.

Jim Mac.—'Tis well.

> (Aside.) I feel that I can trust this coon;
> And yet my mind is sadly ill at ease—
> He seems so faithful; gets his work done
>   soon,
> And always tries his very best to please.
> (To Sam) Tell me now, Sam, who gave yon
>   horse his work?

Sam.—Dat dar new stable-boy done tuk him
  out.

Jim Mac.—You mean the one who always
  tries to shirk

> The rubbing down?—of whom I've had
>   some doubt
> Since first he came?

Sam.—   Yes, sah.

Jim Mac.—   Where is he now?

Sam.—He shootin' craps down yonder by de
  fence.

Jim Mac.—Go send him here

              [Exit Sambonius Niger.]

Jim Mac.—(excitedly).—It would be fine, I
  vow,

> If that kid did some funny work com-
>   mence!

[A voice is heard outside singing. Jimicius listens attentively.]

SONG.

Ta, ra, ra, ra, boom de ay!
Ever since I went away
There's no jockey fit to play;
That's what all the plungers say.
While I did with Britons stay
All my work was very gay:
Wasn't I the boss jock, pray?
Ta, ra, ra, ra, boom de ay!

Jim Mac.—That voice! It must be Toddio
　　returned
　　From far off Albion's shores. I'll call him
　　in.
　　To get his rides my soul now long has
　　yearned. (Goes to stable door.)
　　But lo! he comes.
　　　　　[Enter Toddio Sloanio.]

Tod. Slo.—　　　　How goes it, you old skin?

Jim Mac.—Welcome, my Toddio! (Em-
　　braces him.)　　　　My heart is glad
　　To see my peerless jockey boy once more!
　　Rome heard with joy of triumphs that you
　　had
　　And how your courage made officials sore.

Though some, through spite, your noble
    deeds decried,
And said that you were full of red-hot
    bluff,
Yet will you always be the Romans' pride,
And when it comes to riding, you're the
    stuff!

Tod. Slo.—Come off, Jimicius, don't give me
    taff'!'
I'm not so green as once I used to be.
This guff of yours would make the horses
    laugh;
But it will not go down with Toddio—see?
'Tis true in Albion I cut it fat,
And swiped a "bood" of Britons' rocks as
    well,
And raised some precious rows—but what
    of that?
Stow all that blawsted nonsense, man, and
    tell
This rooster what you want—for well I
    know
You're after something, or you wouldn't
    spout
This balderdash about "your Toddio" so.
Let loose, Jimicius, and fire it out!

Jim Mac.—Ah, cunning Toddio! You are
    so keen   .
    That you divine one's thought before it's
    thought,
    And you can see a thing before it's seen,
    And you can catch a thing before it's
    caught,
    And you can—
Tod. Slo. (impatiently).—Now by all the gods
    I swear,
    Jimicius, let go! or I'll cut stick.
Jim Mac.—Nay, nay, dear Toddio, pray heed
    my prayer;
    I need your aid to help me turn a trick!
Tod. Slo. (aside).—I thought I sized the duf-
    fer up just right.
    He wants a ride. (To Jim Mac.)
                Ha, ha, old buck, I see!
    You've got some "good thing" bottled-up
    all tight
    And would, to cinch it, get a ride from me;
    Is it not so?
Jim Mac.—   Yes, Toddio, right you are.
    I start to-morrow, in the Tiber Stake,
    An untried colt; and he should win as far
    As you can throw a stone, if you will take

The mount. Your stable has no entry in;
So if you're disengaged, why, ride my colt;
I'll guarantee you score another win:
At springing "dark ones" I still "keep my
 holt."
Tod. Slo.—Well, well, Jimicius—let me see—
 I'll think
The matter over, and decide at morn.
Jim Mac.—Nay; say yes now, or I won't
 sleep a wink;
 Don't leave me in this state of doubt for-
  lorn.
 Ride, ride my colt and we will make a
  "coup;"
 You'll drain the cup of glory to the dregs!
 The colt is good; but were he not, 'tis you
 Could make him win, e'en had he but three
  legs!
Tod. Slo.—All right, Jimicius, I guess it goes;
 But I shall want a thousand sesterces
 Cash down before I mount. You see that
  those
 Are my new terms. Besides that, if you
  please,
 You'll have to sign my written guarantee
 Swearing your horse is really good and fit,
 Or else you pay me, should it not thus be,

Five thousand drachmas, furthermore, to
   wit.
You see in Albion I learned some law,
And got my ideas up about these things;
My new agreement's drawn without a flaw:
All owners sign it—not excepting kings.

Jim Mac.—Great Heavens, Toddio your
   terms are high;
Your trip to Albion has made you stiff;
But I will go you. None shall say that I
About his price with Toddio had a tiff.
But some one comes!

   [Enter Sambonius Niger, excited and gasping
   for breath.]

Sam.—　　　　　Good golly! Massa Jim!
Dat boy done say he "fixed" dat two-year
   colt!
He say you win no Tiber Stake wid <u>him</u>!
I try to ketch him, but he make a bolt
And run away!

Jim Mac. (wildly and despairingly).—
　　　　　Great Jove! Lost! All is lost!
That treach'rous boy has robbed me of the
   stake!
If I could catch him, though my life it cost,
I'd every bone within his body break!

Tricked! Fooled again! It almost drives
    me mad!
The gods to ruin me most surely choose!
Now that a mount from Toddio I had
There was no way for me that race to lose!

Tod. Slo. (coolly).—Don't flop up, old Jim-
    icius, but reflect
That though your luck is bad it might be
    worse.
All trainers must these little things expect;
And think what would have happened to
    your purse
If you had not found out this job so soon:
Your colt then would have started quite
    unfit,
And you'd have had to pay me to the tune
Of just five thousand drachmas. So, old
    man,
Let that console you, if there's aught that
    can.
(Going.) I think that I'll be off the town
    toward.
Brace up! Good night!

Jim Mac. (mechanically).—Good night.
                (wildly.)   All lost!

Sam. (mournfully).—   Good Lawd!

(NOTE—In presenting this curious specimen of antique racing history to the reader, it must be understood that the author has modernized to a considerable extent in translating from his fragmentary Latin manuscript. For instance, the song which is sung by Toddio is, in the original, a popular Roman ditty of that day having the refrain,

"Hic, Haec, Hoc, et Hujus Tres!"

the form of which is so similiar to that of "Ta, ra, ra, ra, Boom' de ay," that the author thought it justifiable to render it as given. And so, in translating, with various other points.)

ALL KINDS OF LUCK.

ALL KINDS OF LUCK.

I WAS loafing in the paddock
   On a sizzling summer day,
When the mercury was soaring
   In a most ambitious way;
It had reached about a hundred
And it promised higher yet,
So I'd just about decided
   That it was too hot to bet:

When Jim Jones, who owns "The Fizzer,"
   Came and whispered in my ear:—
"Say, old boy, just keep it quiet
   And I'll give you a good steer;
Tramp's part owner has just told me
   That he'll win beyond a doubt.
Go and put a good bet on it;
   Hurry up!—they're going out."

Now I seldom put my money
   On an ordinary tip,
But I know Jim Jones is "solid,"
   So I made a hurried skip

From the paddock, and I hastened
    To the ring at such hot speed
That the perspiration from me
    Rolled in perfect floods, indeed.

I just glanced across the infield,
    Saw the starter wave his flag,
And I feared that I'd be shut out
    If for odds I tried to lag;
So I cried to the first bookie,
    In a voice that had the cramp,
I was so stewed up and nervous,
    "Here's a hundred! Give me Tramp!"

The young man, a stranger, eyed me
    With a look of mild surprise;
Then he handed down a ticket,
    While a smile was in his eyes.
I did not take time to scan it
    But I crumpled up the thing
And just shoved it in my pocket,
    For "They're off!" rang through the ring.

To the lawn I rushed, and quickly
    Saw with but a single glance
That Tramp's start had spoiled the business
    And he didn't have a chance;

Twenty lengths behind the others
   He was running. I felt sore,
And I walked away disgusted,
   For I cared to see no more.

Well, the race was run and over,
   And Tramp finished in the ruck;
So I pulled out my "dead" ticket,
   With a murmur at my luck.
As I started to destroy it
   Something startling caught my eye;
'Twas "One thousand to one hundred"—
   And I gave a little cry.

I had heard the bookies shouting,
   "Here is Tramp at two to one!"
Just as I had put my bet on,
   When the horses went to run.
Then I narrowly inspected
   My odd ticket, and I saw
It was "Scamp" they'd written on it—
   That "rogue" horse with iron jaw.

"Well," thought I, " it makes no difference,
   For Scamp never could have won;"
When a friend chanced to pass by me
   And I asked him, just in fun,

"Say, who won the race, old fellow?"
    And he answered with a grin,
"Why, 'twas <u>Scamp</u>, that blamed old rascal!
    And his price was 'ten'—to win."

Well, it simply knocked me silly
    And I stood there like a calf;
Then the whole thing seemed so funny
    That I had a hearty laugh;
And, thought I, "Since fate has forced me
    To pull down a bet so rash,
I had best be duly thankful,
    So I'll go and get the cash."

To the ring I gayly ambled
    And I started out to look
For the fellow I had bet with;
    The card read, "Hohokus Book;"
But I couldn't seem to find it,
    Though I went to the same place
Where I entered from the paddock
    When I ran to play the race.

Puzzled greatly, I inquired,
    As a messenger passed by,
If he'd tell me where that book was,
    While my card I let him eye.

"Why!" cried he. "You didn't know it?"
 (By his words my joy was squelched)
It is all around the ring, sir;
 The 'Hohokus Book' has welched!"

Once again was I knocked silly;
 Yet I couldn't help but laugh,
For the whole infernal business
 Seemed to me too rich by half;
And from this most strange experience
 I was by this moral struck—
"Any man who goes a-racing
 Must expect ALL KINDS OF LUCK!"

THE GOODTHING.

—◆ ⸱⸱

HERE is nothing that is better than
a GOODTHING
If the GOODTHING will only go
through.
And everybody likes to get a
GOODTHING;
That is, I do, and so, I think, do you.
When anybody tells me of a GOODTHING
I am grateful and offer him my thanks;
But were I forced to bet on all those GOOD-
THINGS
I could break about a half a dozen banks.

I recollect one time I had a GOODTHING;
I got it from the trainer and the jock;
And it really looked like such a jolly GOOD-
THING
I thought it ought to win "about a block."

So I bet my whole wad calmly on that GOOD-
    THING,
  Though the other horses in the race were
    fast;
Imagine how I felt when my prime GOOD-
    THING
  "Blew up"—and finished absolutely last!

O my friends, let us be "leery" of the GOOD-
    THINGS
  And reflect before we put our money down,
For too much faith in a real, bang up GOOD-
    THING
  Is apt to send us walking back to town.
Now the only thing that <u>really</u> makes a
    GOODTHING,
  As the "wise ones" very frequently have
    said,
Is to "stiffen" all the opposition GOOD-
    THINGS
  And be sure that every other horse is
    "dead."

FELL IN THE STRETCH.

.

FELL IN THE STRETCH.

A CRY bursts forth from the swaying
throng,
A blending of groan and wail;
And faces that were all eager and
flushed
Grow suddenly sad and pale.
A riderless horse comes bounding on,
Swerving round from side to side,
And far away, at the head of the stretch,
Lies the boy who but now did ride.

The other horses come dashing in,
And the race is over and won;
But, even before the wire they've reached
Fifty anxious men have run
Toward the spot where the fallen boy lies still,
And the crowd look more that way
Than they do at the finish of the race,
Though it is the best of the day.

For the hearts of the racing world are soft,
    And you'll have to look hard to find
A gentler man than the thoroughbred sport,
    Or one who is half so kind.
With any trouble or any hurt.
    Or any kind of complaint,
I'd rather go to a racing man
    Than your strait-laced "Charity Saint."

The boy who is down is a favorite,
    And no man or woman there
But would, to help or comfort him,
    Gladly give or do their share;
And so you may hear on every side,
    As you go about the place,
More questions about the injured boy
    Than comments upon the race.

They lift the hurt boy tenderly up
    And bear him gently along,
While the surgeon's quickly at his side
    To examine what is wrong.
Then soon the glad news is given out,
    And flies from lip to lip:
"He's badly hurt, but he'll ride again;
    He'll come round all right this trip!"

And, believe me, nine men out of ten
  Who are gathered at that spot
Will feel just as glad to hear that news
  As if they had "won a pot:"
For a thorough sport would in scorn look
    down
  On a man, as a sordid wretch
Whose heart and cash would not both go out
  To a jock who fell in the stretch.

THE BLIND VETERAN.

THE BLIND VETERAN.

I OFTEN saw upon the stand
    An old, gray bearded man
    Who always sat in one same spot
    Each day the horses ran.
    He never seemed to move about;
He never turned his head
To note the horses in the race
  As round the track they sped.

But still and quiet would he sit,
  Nor cared to watch the race;
His gaze seemed fixed and purposeless,
  Or bent on empty space.
Some time I puzzled why this was,
  Nor could the reason find,
Till, going close to him one day,
  I saw that he was blind.

And then I was with wonder filled
  That such a thing should be,
Why daily this old man should come
  And sit and never see

The stirring scenes which there took place,
  For surely there was naught
Except the <u>sight</u> of such grand sport
  Which there so many brought.

True, there was speculation's charm
  To draw that mighty throng;
But still they came the sport to see,
  With interest all strong.
And hence it struck me as most strange
  And sad, and made me mark
More closely this afflicted man,
  To whom the world was dark.

Close by his side there always stood
  A handsome, bright faced boy,
Who watched each race with gaze intent,
  And seemed to so enjoy
All that took place, I cou'd but feel
  Much interest in the lad,
And often stood there watching him
  When idle time I had.

It chanced that in the stand one day
  I close beside them went
To watch the season's greatest race,
  The turf's supreme event.

Then, even while my eager gaze
  To view the race was strained,
I heard what quickly to my mind
  The mystery explained.

For, from the time the flag went down,
  The boy, in tones all low,
"Called off" the race to the old man,
  That he its course might know.
He "called" the horses as they ran,
  First named the one ahead
And then the others as they came,
  With how much each one led.

'Twas so well done, I could have shut
  My eyes and seen them run.
And only once the old man spoke
  After it was begun.
'Twas when they turned into the stretch,
  And as they straightened out,
When, for a moment, who was first
  E'en caused the lad to doubt.

And, as he paused a moment then
  Until he sure could be—
"Who's leading now? Quick! Tell me, boy!
  My God! that I might see!"

Thus burst the old man's spirit forth,
   And by those words I knew
A tragedy I witnessed there,
   If I divined it true;

For then I felt this veteran
   Was in the sport bound up,
And that it was all dark to him,
   Was his most bitter cup.
So thought I, e'en in that wild din—
   Excitement's maddest whirl:—
"The man who sees and don't thank God,
   Is in good sooth a churl!"

A FAIR ENTHUSIAST.

SHE stood in the stand like an angel
        of light,
    With her dainty hands clasped, as
        in prayer;
    The afternoon breeze (which was
        making me sneeze)
Was playfully rippling her hair;
Her coral-like lips were half parted, as if
    She were murmuring softly and low
Some rapt invocation or soft exclamation;
    Her cheeks with excitement did glow.

Her "eyes like the sea" shone with wonderful
        light
    And her soul seemed to linger in them;
No Orloff nor Kohinoor e'er shone so
        bright—
    Each one was a lustreful gem—-
While her pose, like Diana's, embodied that
        grace

Which the sculptors of old caught so well;
Her form was more beautiful e'en than her
    face,
  And words of its charm fail to tell.

I stood there and gazed unrestrained, for I saw
  That her thoughts were so far from those
    near
That my stare, which exceeded strict cour-
    tesy's law,
  Would not to her notice appear.
Such a vision of loveliness rarely I'd seen,
  Nor one with such soulfulness in,
And I felt but one thing such emotion could
    mean—
  She was "rooting her horse on to win."

THE PIKER'S HYMN.

THE PIKER'S HYMN.

I WANT to be a plunger,
 And with the plungers stand;
A "roll" within my pocket,
 A "wad" within my hand;
And there among the bookies
I'd "pound" with great delight
The horses of my choosing;—
 I hope I'd choose 'em right.

I know it's risky business
 To bet so hard and strong;
I know the biggest cinches
 Quite often go all wrong;
I know that plots of all kinds
 Are sometimes made to smash
The man who "hits it" fiercely
 And puts up "swads" of cash.

I know that little bettors
 Are like the little fish—
They slip out through the meshes
 Which many big ones dish.

Yet all these things don't faze me,
   In bull-head luck I'd trust;
I'd bet 'em to a standstill,
   And either win or bust.

I think of "Jubi' Juggins,"
   Of "Plunger Walton" too;
Their glorious fate I envy—
   Such fortunes to run through!
For what is money made for,
   Except to circulate?
And betting sets it going
   At record breaking gait.

Oh! may I be a plunger,
   And leave "The Piker Class!"
Though people, if I went broke,
   Might "write me down an ass."
But if I won a fortune,
   Great fame would I command;
So let me be a plunger,
   And with the plungers stand!

PETER PFEIFFENSCHNEIDER'S PATRIOTIC "PET."

PETER PFEIFFENSCHNEIDER'S PATRIOTIC "PET."

 GOES me py dot race dracks down
  Vhere all dose horses run;
Mein neffew, Hans, says, "Coom
  along!
"You shoost haf lots of fun!"
·Den vas dot great Soopurpan race,
 Ven efferypotty goes;
Dot crowt vas somedings terrible—
 I schpoils mein Sontag's glose.

Put neffer mindt! Dot vas all righdt;
 I dink dot if I vants
I puys me now some glose als fein
 Als mein young neffew Hans.
Mein pockets shoost is filldt mit cash
 I from dot race did get;
I dells you how I coom to spiel
 Dot batriotic pet.

Ven dot Soopurpan race vas py
  Young Hans he says to me,
"Now, Onkle Peter, you shoost spiel
  Dese vays vot I do—see?
Dot horse I spiels vas favorite,
  He vas so sure to vin;
I puts mein lasdt cent oop on him,
  I vas so certain pin."

Shoost den I sees von horse go py,
  Und dot poy on his pack
He vears dose Deutschen colors oop,
  Shoost like der Deutschen flack;*
Und den I says to Hans, "Mein poy,
  Your Onkle Peter spiels
Dot horse mit Deutschen colors on;
  He batriotic feels."

Und Hans he laughs at me und says,
  "Dot horse no von vill puy;
His price vas 'anydings-you-vant;'
  He von't be ein-zwei-drei."

---

*The colors of W. Gratz, owner of Elkwood, who won
the Suburban of 1888, were a combination very reminis-
cent of the German flag.

"Vell, neffer mindt, mein poy," I says,
    "I vill fife tollars pet;
You go und spiel dot horse for me,
    Shoost now, alretty yet."

So Hans mein money dakes und goes,
    Und cooms pack right avay
Und says, "Vell, Onkle, you vas on,
    Put you vas voon pig jay!
Dot Deutschen horse vill neffer do—
    He vill not get ein schmell.
Drei hoondredt to your fiife I got."
    I shoost says, "Very vell."

Dot race soon vas off; put I
    Dose horses could not see;
I vas so short und schtout, you know,
    Dot crowt shoost shumps on me.
Put ven dey coom dot finish py
    Von moment I could look,
Und den I see dot Deutschen horse
    Vas "All der money took!"

I schlaps young Hans right on der pack
    Und says, "Now, vat you dink
Of Onkle Peter, Hans, mein poy?
    Let's go und dake ein trink!"

Und Hans he only says, "Mein Gott!
  Der Deutsch vas great for luck!
I no more dinks dot horse could vin—
  I vas py lightnings struck!"

Vell, neffer mindt!   I gets mein cash
  Und puts it safe avay.
I spiels no more; it machts nichts aus
  Vot anypotty say.
I know dose races I can't peat;
  Put shoost for vonce I get
Der pest of dem pecause I makes
  Von batriotic pet!

MICKEY McMANUS.
AND HIS
"FARRUM STHUDY."

MICKEY M'MANUS

AND HIS

"FARRUM STHUDY."

E jabers! Dhese harses wud dhrive a
man crazy!
Dhere's niver a wan av thim runs
loike he shud.
Oi've figgered thim out till me moind
is all hazy,
An' me brains is as t'ick as ould Galway's
foine mud.

Oi've sthudied me "Goide" an' the farrum in
the poipers;
Oi've sthudied the handicap shystem as
well;
But the divilish bastes all indoolge in such
coipers
That sorra a t'ing can a dacent man tell.

'Twas a few days ago "Bridget" won very aisy
  In company good an' in toime very fasht;
Thin to-day she stharts out an' runs murther-
    in' lazy—
  In a field av old crabs shure she runs about
    lasht!

Oi figgered "Tim Murphy" a cinch an' a
    moral—
  For a month he was "placed" ivery toime he
    did sthart—
But the toime that I backed him the bloody
    ould sorrel
  Runs loike he was dhrawin' a waterin' cart.

Dhere was ould "Billy Baker," a baste that
    cud niver
  Run half fast enough for to kape himsilf
    warrum,
An' he comes out an' bates as foine harses as
    iver
  Were figgered as winners on ivery day
    farrum.

An' thin dhere's a crackerjack they call
"The Flier."
On a Monday he'll win, on a Chewsday he'll
lose,
An' win agin Wednesday! The divil admire
Such an in-an'-out baste! Shure it do give
wan the blues!

Oi've given it up—an 'Oi've burnt me ould
dope-book;
Oi've put by me "Goide" on the very top
shilf.
Av Oi kipt on Oi'd be loike the man who a
rope took
To make his cravat—Oi'd be hangin' me-
silf! .

THE TRACK IN WINTER.

THE TRACK IN WINTER.

THE gates were all closed and the ring
  was deserted,
 The grand stand was empty, the
  "rail birds" had flown,
While through the bare trees which
  the outer rail skirted
 The winter wind whistled with
  desolate moan.

The snowflakes were falling and spreading a
  carpet
 Of white o'er the track's broad, smooth
  ribbon of brown;
Ere long they would bury it up to the railtops
 If they kept on coming so steadily down.

The stables seemed lifeless and cheerless and
  empty,
 Except three or four, where a gray smoke
  arose
To show that some horses there kept winter
  quarters—
 The only warm spot in a picture of snows.

I lingered a moment and viewed the scene
    sadly,
  As I thought of the life which but lately was
    there;
Then whipped up my horse and drove on again
    briskly,
  My sleigh bells all tinkling a farewell to care.

"For," thought I, "it is foolish to mourn o'er
    the present
  When it is unpleasant, and surely won't last,
And when one considers a race track in winter
  He should look to its future, or turn to its
    past."